SILENT KNIGHT

REIGNING HEARTS
BOOK 2

EVIE MITCHELL

THUNDER THIGHS PUBLISHING

Editor: Nicole Wilson, Evermore Editing
http://www.evermoreediting.wixsite.com/info
Cover: Laras Putri

ACKNOWLEDGEMENT OF COUNTRY

I acknowledge the Traditional Custodians of the lands on which I write, the Ngunnawal people, and pay my respect to elders both past and present.

I acknowledge the continued and deep spiritual relationship of the Australian Aboriginal and Torres Strait Islander peoples' to this land, and their unique cultural and spiritual relationships to the land, waters and seas and their rich contribution to society.

Always was, always will be.

AUTHOR NOTE

My Dearest Greedy Reader,

Thank you for choosing to read Silent Knight!

Trigger warnings are listed as follows:

Rejected by fiancé, public embarrassment, dirty talk, consensual sex.

If you have any concerns, please email me at. EvieMitchellAuthor@gmail.com

I went to hide—and found my heart instead.

Charlotte

Being a princess sucks. Everyone expects you to display grace, poise, and beauty. They expect a prince to sweep you off your feet and happily ever afters.

No one wants to hear about the Prince who turns out to be a toad. Or see you toss wedding cake in said Prince's face.

When I'm unceremoniously dumped by my fiancé, I suddenly become a media must-have. Hounded by the press, I'm left with no choice but to hide out in the last place anyone expects to find me.

Polar Bear, Alaska.

I expected to find solitude and peace, maybe lick my wounds by eating ice cream from the carton and watching Love, Actually on repeat.

I didn't expect Croydon 'Roy' Knight.

He's gruff. He's surly. He hates all things Christmas.

He's also the most real man I've ever met.

And for some reason, I'm deeply attracted to him.

Could it be...? Could I have found my Knight in tarnished armour?

ONE
CHARLOTTE

**Astipian Kingdom, Isle of Astipia
Princess Charlotte's Bedroom, Royal
Palace**

"It's in all the papers."

"And social media is having a field day," my brother bemoaned from somewhere above me.

"This is a calamity. Shall I issue a press release?"

I tried to block out the voices of my family and employees standing around the bed. Stubbornly, I pressed my face into my pillow, determined to stay cocooned under the blankets for all eternity.

If I ignore them, they'll go away.

"Charlotte, my love, you need to deal with this," my mother coaxed. "Come out from under the blankets."

Booger.

"I don't want to," I muttered into the silk of my pillowcase. "Go away."

"What did she say? Did she say no?" Someone—my brother, no doubt—began to tug at the blanket. "Charlotte, let go. We need to deal with this."

"No." I hung on for dear life. "Go away."

"Leo, leave her," Mother admonished. "She's grieving."

The mattress dipped beside me, my body rolling toward the depression. Even from under the blanket I could smell mother's familiar perfume. I drew in a deep breath, taking comfort from the subtle scent of rose water and cinnamon.

"Charlotte." My mother placed a warm hand on my back. "Come out, darling. Speak to us."

I adored my family, don't get me wrong. But all I wanted to do was crawl into a hole and lick my wounds. I had no desire to talk about what had to be the most embarrassing moment for this family in many a generation—and that was saying something considering one of my great-grandparents declared war on a country that didn't exist.

"A princess never hides, Lottie. She faces the world head-on."

Ugh.

With a resigned sigh, I rolled over, peeking out from under the weighted blanket. "I don't like you very much right now."

"We know." Mother reached over, running a hand across my hair. "But we're here to help."

I groaned, dropping my head back to the pillow, staring up at the canopy of my bed.

Last night I thought I'd never sleep under it again. And now look at me. Hiding like a child.

I screwed my eyes shut. "This is so embarrassing."

"It's not your embarrassment to hold. It is completely his."

I blew out a wet laugh, tears stinging the backs of my eyes. "We both know that a man is rarely vilified in these kinds of situations." I rose on my elbows, finding my brother hovering anxiously near the bed. "Let me guess, the narrative is that I'm not woman enough to have kept—" I stumbled over my ex-fiancé's name. "Frederick?"

Leo winced, his tawny gaze skittering away,

a flush darkening his cheeks. "Not entirely. But—"

I sighed, closing my eyes. "I knew it."

"We can fix this," my press secretary said, dropping to a seat beside the bed. "You're the wronged party. We can—"

I heard a commotion outside my bedroom—angry voices followed by a clatter. For a moment my heart leapt as I imagined Frederick storming into the room to lie prone at my feet, declaring his love for me as he begged me to take him back.

I wouldn't take him back, of course. But it would do my pride a great service to see him so apologetic.

"I will *murder* him!"

My sister, the Queen, waddled into the room, one hand resting on her pregnant belly, the other pointed at Leo. "Call the Minister for Defence. Call the Prime Minister. We're declaring war on Morocco."

A shadow of a smile graced my lips, warm gooeyness pooling in my belly. "Kit, a war isn't necessary."

"Oh," she said, halting at the foot of my bed. "I can absolutely assure you it is."

"She's hungry," Jonathan, her husband, explained, joining the crowd. "She needs to eat."

"I do not. I need to fuck up the man who—"

He handed her a cookie, pressing a kiss to her forehead. "Eat, Queenie. You can declare war after we get those sugar levels up."

She glared at him as she took a bite, her jaw moving furiously as she chewed.

The handsome ex-politician adored my sister, and I adored him for his love of her. Katherine had inherited the crown from my father upon his death, and for many years I'd fretted that she'd never let anyone into her heart. She'd been so lost in her duty to our people, that anything even remotely constituting an emotion had been locked away —hidden from the pressures of the world.

Until Jon. Seeing her trip into love had been its own kind of blessing. Watching her lose all sense of propriety with this pregnancy had delighted the entire family.

The child, we were convinced, would be a hellhound.

"Better?" Jon asked, his fingers tangling in my sister's dark hair.

"Maybe."

Amusement hovered like a shadow, the barest hint of it touching my shame.

Watching Kit and Jon interact, I was reminded of their wedding day. Watching my beautiful sister perform the traditional marriage dance with her groom had been a privilege I would hold dear for the rest of my life.

Yet another example of why your own marriage was doomed from the start.

My fiancé had refused to learn our customary dance and had politely but firmly refused to wear our tribe's traditional wedding attire—despite knowing how important it was to me.

He professed to love you and yet didn't bother to learn a single thing about you.

All the small voices I'd suppressed for months rose as one, the choir of doubts I'd stubbornly willed away now finding footholds.

Did he ever love me? Did he ever even care?

"Berryn?" My mother asked, turning to the short man seated beside my bed. "Thoughts?"

My press secretary straightened, his lips pursed, a frown marring his brow as he considered my options.

Berryn was young for a press secretary, but I'd hired him for that youth. When considering who would look after my diary and interactions, I'd wanted someone who understood the importance of engaging on the platforms where people were. I wanted someone who cared about what I cared about—climate change, good policy, supporting the fight against inequality and racism. And the young Manari man more than met the brief.

Berryn swallowed. "We could release a statement stating it was a mutual decision—"

Leo snorted, crossing his arms over his chest.

"—though we should expect Frederick to counter noting that he... he...." He trailed off.

"You can say it." I sat up, the blanket dropping to pool in my lap. "He ran out."

The words flopped into the middle of the room with all the grace of a piglet performing ballet, my statement placing a freeze on its inhabitants.

"He ran out on me during a worldwide televised ceremony. And I—" I sucked in a breath. "I followed him to toss cake in his stupid face."

"Stupid is an understatement," Kit muttered, her hands rubbing across her distended stomach.

I looked down at my dress, the beautiful bespoke wedding dress that had held so many hopes and dreams in each stitch and seam.

Why am I still wearing it?

"Well," my mother said, her tone light. "I would say you had reasons to act with less restraint than is normally appropriate."

"Reasons?" Leo barked, running hands through his dark hair. "Mother, the bastard—"

"Berryn," I interrupted, weary of this conversation. "Be straight with us. What are the best options?"

"We release a statement and then you, temporarily, retreat."

Jon coughed, drawing our attention.

"Retreat how exactly?" He gestured at the windows on the far side of my room. One of the maids had thoughtfully drawn the curtains, blocking out any possibility of someone witnessing this conversation.

"The palace has been mobbed by reporters. The entire Kingdom is in uproar—not to mention all the royal fans internationally. The King of Morocco is threatening to disown his kin."

And therein lay the crux of my issues. Being a princess required decorum. It required poise and grace. It required one to rise above petty emotion and put the future of the country first.

It did not allow for the throwing of cake in the face of lying, cheating fiancés—no matter how well deserved.

"I have an idea." Berryn paused, looking meaningfully at the gathered crowd in my room.

In addition to Berryn and my family, guards hovered in each corner, staff fluttered around, and—for some reason—a gardener held a bouquet as he leaned against my bathroom door.

Mother rose, the epitome of style and grace in her mother-of-the-bride plum-coloured morning dress.

Yet another relic of the wedding-that-will-never-be.

"If the family might have some privacy?" she asked, though her tone brooked no protests.

The staff stepped from the room, the gardener closing the door behind him.

Alone with the Royal family, Berryn flushed—appearing suddenly tongue-tied.

"Out with it," Kit said, her hand rubbing circles on her belly. "Hurry now."

"Croydon Knight."

My heart kicked, my belly dipping. Mother sucked in a breath, her face pinching. I reached out, clasping her hand in my own.

"He's my cousin," Berryn hurried on. "And, as you know, imminently qualified to protect her Highness."

"Who is he?" Jon asked, registering the change in the room.

"Father's ex-bodyguard. After his death, I

offered Croydon the head security position but he—" Kit swallowed. "He decided to retire instead."

Jon frowned. "It was a fraught parting?"

"On the contrary," Mother whispered, letting go of my hand to brush a stray tear from her cheek. "Roy's loss was greatly felt."

I swallowed. "It's because of him that Daddy's illness wasn't leaked to the press. His ruthlessness meant Father was able to announce the news in his own time."

There was a beat of silence as we remembered that hard period of our lives.

Father's illness had been a long, slow ending to his otherwise vibrant life. Our family had lived with the grief of knowing he would be gone long before we'd announced his terminal illness to the public.

Roy's determination had delivered the one thing of which my family had so little—privacy.

"He's a good man." Leo reached out to touch my leg. "He'll ensure you get the time you need to heal."

"Our family owes a great deal to Croydon Knight." Mother dapped at her face with a handkerchief. "I'm not sure he would be willing to take on this duty."

"He already agreed."

I stared at Berryn, my hope rising.

"But on one condition."

"Anything," I said.

"He'll only do it if you go to him."

I cocked an eyebrow. "And where exactly is he?"

"Polar Bear, Alaska."

TWO
CHARLOTTE

Polar Bear, Alaska

A *Princess never curses.*

The rule had been drilled into me since birth. But had I not been a princess, I would have described the air as colder than a polar bear's tit. I'd have sworn black and blue, questioning every being who had thought living in this environment was a good idea.

Who enjoyed the cold? Honestly, who?

Instead, I did what any good princess does, and coughed politely to signal my discomfort.

"It's a tad... cold."

The private jet had touched down on the quiet airfield, jostling me from my sleep.

Wrapped in a thick jumper and insulated pants, I'd not expected the pilot to be quite so quick to open the doors.

"It's twenty-eight below."

I swallowed. "Is that Fahrenheit or Celsius?"

Behind me, Berryn snorted. "Does it matter?"

The older pilot grabbed my bags. "The car's across the runway. I'll meet you there."

I shivered as he disappeared out into the gently swirling snow.

"Berryn?"

"Yes, Highness?"

I wrapped my arms around myself, shuddering as the cold air stung my cheeks. "Are we sure this is a good idea?"

He sighed his breath a cloud of steam. "It's the only one we have."

We collected my remaining bags and then stepped from the jet, both of us gasping in the frigid air. The cold stung my eyes, hiding the sudden tears as a wave of homesickness hit me.

I missed Astipia. Despite being located in the North Atlantic, my island home experienced sultry summers and mostly mild winters. Only the northern islands received decent snow during winter, with tourists flocking to the renowned snow fields. Rarely did I wish to be anywhere near that level of freezing temperature. As much as Hollywood touted the magic of white Christmases snuggled by the fire, I couldn't see the appeal.

Snow in my hair. Wind in my face. Wet, cold feet. No, thank you. Give me a day on a beach every year.

Miserable, cold, and full of self-pity, I cursed Frederick for this mess as I followed Berryn across the snow-covered runway to a waiting black SUV.

A man stood at the trunk, watching us.

Oh.

Croydon Knight wore a thick black coat, chunky winter boots, and dark-wash winter pants. On his head sat a beanie that should have looked ridiculous but instead added to his good looks.

Good looks?

I faltered, my heart skipping a beat.

Pull it together, Charlotte. You're here to heal and hide. Not jump in bed with a man who looks like he wrestles bears before breakfast.

Once upon a time, I'd entertained a crush on the handsome bodyguard. But that had disappeared when Frederick had swept me off my feet.

I sucked in a breath, the cold air slapping me back to reality.

I'm here to heal, not rekindle an old crush.

The pilot finished throwing my bags in the trunk in a manner I could only describe as cavalier.

As Roy watched on, the pilot slammed the boot shut, dusting his hands.

"Refuel, then we leave for Anchorage in an hour," the pilot told Berryn. "I'll meet you in the lounge."

Berryn nodded, hunkering in his overly large coat.

"Cousin."

Roy lifted his head in acknowledgement.

Around us, the wind howled, and the snow fell as Roy considered me.

I awkwardly bounced from foot to foot, waiting for someone to tell me what to do.

With a sigh, Roy flicked a hand at the passenger door.

"Get in."

"What, not even a hello for your cousin?" Berryn asked with a laugh. "Surely we could get coffee."

"Not when you're interrupting my peace." Roy rounded the car. "I'll see you in April. Tell your mother I said hello, and her son is terrible."

I winced as he slammed the door shut.

Berryn turned to me, stuffing his hands into his parker pockets. "Ignore him. He's always like this during the winter months. I think he's related to a bear."

I tried for a weak smile.

"Do you have everything you need?"

I nodded. "Thank you. For everything."

My press secretary shrugged. "It's my job."

And there lay the saddest part of my life. This wasn't a friendship. I paid him to do this.

"Well, thank you. I appreciate it."

He held the passenger door open, guiding me in.

"Stay safe, Highness."

I nodded, clutching my bag to my chest. "You too."

The door closed, sealing me in with a man I hadn't seen in over five years.

With a bracing breath, I twisted, pasting my brightest smile on my face.

"Croydon, it's great to—"

"Don't." He hit a button, the car rumbling to life under us.

"I—"

"Just sit in silence. I need to concentrate."

I snapped my mouth closed, a flush working its way up my neck.

He doesn't want you here.

With a silent curse at Fredrick, I clicked on my seat belt and mentally zipped my lips. In silence, we left the airport, disappearing into the snowy wilderness.

THREE

CHARLOTTE

Polar Bear, Alaska

About an hour outside the airport, I finally cracked. Anxious, jet-lagged, and overwhelmed by the acres of space, snow, and sky, I needed reassurance.

"Roy, where are we going?"

He grunted. "To my cabin."

"Where is that?"

"Polar Bear."

"It's in the town?"

He shook his head, reaching up to pull off his beanie. "A few clicks outside. You'll be safe there."

I settled back in my seat, my leg jiggling nervously as I watched Roy navigate the icy roads.

He'd aged since I'd last seen him at Father's funeral. Lines now touched the corners of his eyes, and a rugged black beard covered his once clean-shaven face, the colour only a few shades darker than his hair. I remembered his grey eyes, steely and with the power to see all your secrets. But I'd forgotten how beautiful they were when paired with his luscious mouth. I couldn't quite tell because he still wore his thick jacket, but I had my suspicion that he'd added more bulk to his already impressive body. He reminded me of a mountain man, wild and carefree.

Or at least he had been—before I'd crashed the party.

"You tell anyone you were headed here?"

I shook my head.

"Good." He relaxed a fraction, his hands loosening their grip on the steering wheel.

He drove in silence for a few more kilometres.

"While you're here, we'll call you Charlie."

"Charlie?"

He sent me a side-long glance. "Can't be called Your Highness if you want to keep a low profile."

"Oh, of course not."

I mentally repeated the nickname.

Charlie. Okay. I can do this.

"Will we be meeting a lot of people?"

He snorted. "No."

I waited for more information, silently sighing when he didn't continue.

"Are we stopping in town?"

"No."

"Should I—"

"No."

I shut my mouth, turning to stare out the window at the wild landscape around us. I remember Roy as being direct, but kind. This felt almost antisocial.

Maybe he's just nervous.

And if he isn't?

Then this is going to be a long month....

———

"When you said a few clicks out of town, I wasn't expecting this."

The fading light reflected off the heaped snow bordering the small cabin. In the distance, the sea glinted, the lights of the nearby town of Polar Bear twinkling in the shadows of the mountains that surrounded it.

Roy's house sat far up in the mountains, miles from any signs of civilization. He was clearly a man who didn't want company.

I stepped from the SUV, the air

immediately stinging my naked skin like a million pinpricks.

I hunched over, tucking my face into my jacket. In the dying light, I glanced around, stunned by the silence of the area.

Is this heaven? Or hell?

Snow crunched, warning me of Roy's approach.

"This way."

He led me up the path, my bags tucked under his arms.

I trailed him feeling a little like a lost duckling.

"Have you lived here long?" I ventured, desperate to fill the silence.

"Long enough."

I gritted my teeth, determined to hold on to my positivity even as I trudged through cold, wet, piles of snow to his front porch.

If this had been a couple's weekend away, I'd have fallen in love with the brick and wood exterior of his cabin. I'd have romanticised the various adorable touches that reminded me of a storybook—but alas, I had no happily ever after.

I frowned, shoving away all thoughts of Frederick the dick.

Roy shoved the door open, and I followed,

sucking in a breath as I paused in the doorway, staring at the magnificent interior.

Pale wood met polished stone in a symphony of architecture. The small space felt large thanks to a vaulted ceiling and giant, insulated windows.

"This is beautiful." I reached out to trail fingers against the softwood walls.

A clatter of nails against the stone floor alerted me to incoming movement. A flash of white fur was all the warning I had before a giant dog leapt onto my chest, pushing me back into the door, a tongue lapping enthusiastically at my face.

"Phoebe, down!" Roy snapped, the dog immediately dropping to sit at my feet, her giant tail sweeping across the floor.

"Oh," I whispered, dropping to my knees to run fingers through her thick fur. "You're gorgeous."

The dog rolled onto her belly, her gigantic body wiggling in rapturous joy.

"Leave her. I'll show you the bedroom."

In his gruff, silently disapproving way, Roy led me through the house—with Phoebe trailing us—pointing out the various rooms and features.

"Fireplace."

"Bathroom."

"Kitchen."

"Deck."

"Master Bedroom."

We paused in the doorway to his massive master suite, my heart skipping a small beat.

Windows dominated two of the four walls of the room, showcasing the expanse of wilderness outside. The high roof allowed for a sense of grandeur, but the warm wood panelling and cheerful fireplace made it feel warm and homely. He owned a massive bed, the generous mattress covered in thick, fluffy blankets.

I may hate the snow, but I could see myself in that bed. I'd sleep in, only to wake to a roaring fire and fresh cocoa which I'd sip while reading the latest Megan Wade romance novel.

A girl had her priorities.

"Wow. I can't wait to see my room."

"This is it."

I blinked, tilting my head back to stare up at him. "Sorry?"

His grey eyes met mine, his expression unreadable.

"W-what," I stammered, my heart pounding. "What do you mean? I can't take your room."

He broke eye contact, turning to nod at the bed. "You're not. We're sharing."

"What?"

His jaw tightened. "I've only got one bed, Princess. Take it or leave it."

I stared at this man I used to know, all thoughts flying from my head as I attempted to process this news.

Oh, dear.

FOUR
ROY

Polar Bear, Alaska

I watched Charlotte's big brown eyes blink rapidly, her face unable to hide her emotions.

I see you, Princess.

My gut tightened, awaiting her response.

When Berryn had called to ask this favour I should have said no. No, I should have said *fuck* no, and then changed numbers.

This is a terrible idea.

For a decade I'd served as a bodyguard to the King of Astipia. I'd been privy to his family, to his friends, to moments that would mark history long after I'd turned to ash.

I'd loved every moment of my work—except for her.

Princess Charlotte.

She'd been eighteen when I'd joined the King's Service. Bright eyed, and a compelling mix of innocent and world-weary, she'd brought me cookies on my first day.

"She makes them herself, you know." The King had told me, pride in his voice as he took one from the plate. "She's a good girl, my Lottie. Smart, gracious, kind but with a backbone. She makes this old man proud."

As their father's illness had progressed, Princess Katherine had taken on more responsibility in the day-to-day running of the Kingdom, while Charlotte had seen to their father. They'd spent hours together while she looked after him, supporting him through state visits and diplomatic discussions—taking some of the pressure away from the ailing King.

And all the while I'd been forced to watch this bud of a girl bloom into an incredible woman—the kind of woman that in any other life I'd have dated, taken to bed, and married.

But one didn't fall for their client. And a bastard from the rough end of town didn't marry a Princess.

"One bed?" she asked, her face flushing. "What about the couch?"

"Phoebe sleeps there."

Charlotte's hands locked in front of her.

The decade I'd spent protecting the Monarch had given me ample opportunity to catalogue this woman's expressions. I knew when she was nervous. I knew when she was hungry. I knew when she was bored, or interested, happy or sad.

I knew she loved dogs and the sun. I knew she wore socks to bed. I knew she loved old sitcoms and romance novels. I knew she laughed when she felt intimidated and cried when she was happy.

And I knew that she locked her hands in front of her when she was nervous.

Good. You should be.

I knew a million things about this woman but one question continued to plague me.

I wonder what she tastes like.

And fuck, did I want an answer to that question.

I watched her rock on her heels, considering my comment.

"Will we—" She coughed into her closed fist. "That is—I mean to say—um—"

"Spit it out, Princess."

"I've never slept with anyone before."

I blinked. "Never?"

Charlotte flushed, dropping her gaze to the floor. "I don't mean it in a bad way. Just warning you that I might snore or sleep talk or be a kicker. I'm not sure."

"Pause. Rollback. You've *never* slept with anyone? But you were engaged."

She blew out a breath. "I know. Maybe that should have been a red flag. But at the time I thought he was being considerate of our lack of privacy as two very public people."

She glanced up, her lips twisted into a self-deprecating smile. "More fool me, right?"

Red hot desire flushed through my body as I experienced a near overwhelming need to kiss her, to hold her, to prove to her that she wasn't the fool. For the first time in my life, I worried that my control might snap.

I stepped back, shutting down the conversation.

"Make yourself at home." I turned on my heel, heading to the back deck.

"Where are you going?"

"To chop wood."

Maybe physical labour would help me regain some sense.

I pictured Charlotte's curvy body, her big dark eyes, her rich chestnut hair, and her full, bow-shaped lips.

I swore under my breath.

"Un-fucking-likely."

FIVE

ROY

Polar Bear, Alaska

After an hour or two of manual labour, I felt like I had enough of a handle on my emotions to return to the cabin. Big mistake.

I stepped through the back door, stomping ice from my boots as the scent of cookies hit me and Christmas music filled my ears.

I found Charlotte in the kitchen, dancing as she piped icing sugar onto cooling baked goods.

"What the fuck?"

Her head lifted, her smile wide and genuine. It felt like a punch to the guts. The last hour's work went up in smoke as my mouth watered with the need to taste her tawny skin.

"You're back!" She lifted a plate, holding it out to me. "Cookie?"

I glanced down at the pile, noting the variety of holiday-themed goods.

"I don't eat cookies," I lied, desperate not to succumb to her charms. "Let alone those that look like Christmas decorations."

"Don't you like Christmas?"

"Fuck no."

Her eyes narrowed. "What about cookies? Don't tell me you don't eat cookies."

I shook my head.

"You did when you were at that Palace."

I cocked an eyebrow. "Did I?"

She blinked, her lips pressing together. "Never? You've never eaten cookies?"

I shook my head again.

"Not even—?"

"No."

She sighed, dropping the plate on my counter. "I'm sure you were a delightful child."

I snorted.

"No Christmas cookies. Honestly. The elves must weep for your soul."

"Probably." I dropped onto one of my bar stools, unable to keep my distance.

"You know, Christmas cookies are good luck." She picked up the makeshift piping bag she'd Macgyvered together with what looked like a plastic bag and a paper straw, resuming her decorating. "If you eat one, they grant wishes."

I crossed my arms, amused by the conversation. "They do, do they?"

"Uh-huh." She finished with a flourish and moved on to the next cookie. "And when made by a princess they're extra-extra lucky."

"That so?"

She sent me a teasing look. "They grant you your heart's deepest desire."

Unable to stop myself, I shoved one in my mouth, humouring her.

Vanilla, cinnamon, and a touch of nutmeg exploded on my tongue; the buttery perfection sweet but perfectly balanced.

"Fuck," I muttered, slowing my chew to savour the taste.

"Good?"

"Great," I corrected, swallowing and reaching for another. "But I still hate Christmas."

She pointed at my cabin. "I can tell. No Christmas decorations? Roy, we're in December. Christmas is only days away."

I grunted, shoving another cooking in my mouth to keep from speaking.

She watched me chew with a small grin.

"I'm glad you had everything on hand for me to bake these. I didn't think a man like you would have icing sugar."

I stilled, watching her continue to pipe.

Whipped. That's what I was. Whipped and a complete jackass. I'd gone shopping with the express purpose of building a pantry I knew she'd utilise while here.

She glanced up a pleased grin on her face. "What did you wish for? What's your heart's greatest desire?"

You.

I cleared my throat. "World peace?"

She laughed, sending her hair tumbling over her shoulders. "Try again."

"A vacation to Australia."

She lifted an eyebrow. "I thought you'd wish for the Lions to win the Astipia cup."

She'd remembered.

I relaxed on my barstool. "You never were a football fan."

"Sportsball isn't for me."

I winced. "Sportsball? Really, Charlie?"

She paused at my use of her new nickname. "I never got the appeal. I'd sit listening to you and Father talk about these matches as if you were playing it yourself." Her expression grew wistful. "He did love a good football game."

I reached out, squeezing her arm. "He was a good man."

"The best," she agreed, her eyes watery. "It's hard not to miss him."

We fell silent, remembering the old King.

"Why did you leave?"

I glanced up, finding her watching me.

"Did you hate your job so much? Or was it us? Did we do something wrong?"

The tremor in her voice hit me right in the gut.

"No, never." I sucked in a breath. "I just needed to do something different." The lie fell easily from my tongue.

"Moving halfway around the world to live in a cabin by yourself is certainly that."

"I don't live here full time. Just part of the year."

"What do you do the rest of it?" she asked, moving to the sink and beginning to wash up.

I rose, reaching for a dishcloth to assist.

"Security advisor. Mostly movie stars and billionaires trying to avoid stalkers or disgruntled customers or staff."

I accepted her offered bowl, drying the washed crockery.

"But why here?" She gestured at the window. "It's so far away."

Exactly. Here, there's no chance of running into you.

I shrugged. "Seemed as good as anywhere."

She accepted that without comment.

We washed and dried in companionable silence.

"I'm sorry for intruding on your privacy," she said softly, her head lifting to look at me. "I know you're not happy about it."

"What gives you that impression?"

She shrugged. "Your welcome wasn't exactly... welcoming."

I swallowed guilt a bitter taste in my mouth.

"That wasn't about you."

Her eyebrows lifted.

"I had to make sure we weren't followed. I was in work mode."

She processed that, turning back to begin cleaning a plate. "Oh."

More truths hovered on my tongue, desperate to be set free.

And I hate knowing your stay isn't permanent. I fucking hate knowing I can't keep you.

"Sorry," I grunted, uncomfortable with this conversation. "If I made you feel uncomfortable."

"You didn't."

I had, but she'd never admit it.

"So," I said, determined to break the awkwardness between us. "Wanna tell me what happened to bring you to a shack in the middle of nowhere?"

She groaned, her head dropping forward, her hair covering her cheeks. "'Berryn didn't tell you?"

"Something about the fiancé now being an ex-fiance. Wanna elaborate?"

"No."

"Come on," I cajoled, hip bumping her. "It can't be that bad."

"Oh, Roy. How do you not know?" She looked up, her face flushed. "It's all over the news."

I gestured around the cabin. "No TV. I've been here for months."

Mostly avoiding any news of you.

"What about the internet?"

I shrugged. "Not much for dealing with technology while here. I check the weather but that's it. This place is about disconnection."

She nodded, worrying her lower lip.

"Come on, tell me."

"I threw cake in a man's face," she blurted out.

I froze.

"On international television."

My eyebrows lifted.

"After he walked out on me. On my wedding day."

A red haze dropped over my vision.

"He did what?"

She blew out a sigh. "And told me, in front of all our guests, the priest, the Gods, and the millions of billions of watchers around the world that... that...." She sucked in a breath.

"That *what*?" I growled.

"That I wasn't good enough for him."

I put down the dishcloth, turning on my heel to head for the door.

"Roy? Roy! Where are you going?"

Calmly I reached for my coat, shrugging it on. "To the airport."

"What?" Charlotte stared at me; her eyes wide. "Why?"

"'I need to assassinate a Moroccan prince."

A startled laugh burst from between her lips, her hand clapping over her mouth as amused delight danced in her eyes. "Roy!"

I ignored her, my mind on the logistics of carrying out the killing.

She'd have to come, of course. I couldn't leave her here unprotected. I'd need to hire a private plane and organise temporary protection for her while I did the deed. An untraceable gun would be required. And a legitimate excuse to be in the same country as the fucker. But all of those were easily dealt with. By tomorrow the bastard would be—

"Roy!" She reached out, halting my movement. "Stop. He's not worth a life sentence."

"But you are."

Charlotte froze. "What?"

I leaned down, getting in her space. The smell of sugar and vanilla clung to her, the innocent scent a balm to my rage.

"You're worth it, Charlotte. And if that fucker can't see it—if he felt that leaving you was a viable option, then he doesn't deserve to live."

Her eyes widened, her mouth forming a small o. "Roy?"

I grunted. "What?"

She rested a hand on the space above my heart, her palm warm through my shirt.

"Kiss me."

Polar Bear, Alaska

I'd never asked a man to kiss me before. I could hear my numerous deportment teachers screaming silently at me from across the ocean.

A princess must demonstrate restraint. She must be chaste. She must be conservative. She must never show emotion. She must, she must, she must.

I was tired of must. Bone-deep-soul-weary of must and need and have-to. I'd lived with these rules my entire life, following each one diligently since I was old enough to walk.

I'd done everything right. I'd dated the right man. I'd attended the right parties. I'd been quiet and demure and gracious and boring.

Yes, boring.

That is exactly what I'd been. I'd been bored with who I was and what I did. Utterly bored with life and the regime, and chaffing until the weight of others' expectations.

I wanted to be a rebel. I wanted to break rules—and Roy's statement awakened a hereto unknown rebelliousness within me.

I wanted to be naughty.

"Kiss me," I repeated, shifting closer to him. "Please, Roy."

For a beat, I thought he'd throw me off, giving me a cute pat on the head and a patronising smile.

I braced myself, steeling my emotions for the coming rejection.

At least I tried.

But with a shuddered groan, Roy's hands delved into my hair, holding my head still. I blinked, a small gasp slipping free a fraction before his lips covered mine.

Ohhh...!

His kiss felt like a revelation.

Hot and hungry, he devoured me, setting my body on fire.

Oh. Oh. Oh.

His mouth never leaving mine, he dipped slightly, his hands boosting me up. Automatically, I wrapped arms and legs around him like a greedy koala, plastering our bodies together.

He walked us towards the wall, my back moulding to the smooth wood, his hardness merging with my soft curves.

This is... wow.

Growling with satisfaction, Roy renewed his efforts, nipping and sucking at my lips until I opened for him. Pushing his advantage, his tongue tasted and teased, driving hot shards of desperate need through my belly.

Oh. This is what a kiss is meant to be. How have I lived without this?

When I'd met Frederick, I'd done the right thing. I'd allowed him to woo me, I'd fallen under his clever, witty, charismatic spell. I'd done exactly what was asked of me by finding a suitable match who checked all the boxes—rich, media trained, appropriate linage, no skeletons in the closet.

The Palace had been thrilled.

And I'd been happy, for a while. If I were honest, I'd even fancied myself in love.

But something had always been missing from our relationship. I'd wanted hungry kisses when all he offered were chaste pecks. I'd wanted groping hands and desperate words when all I'd received were gentle hugs and pretty compliments.

I'd resigned myself to the assumption that romance novels and movies had lied about love. It might be a many splendid thing, but it wasn't fireworks and pops of colour. My love was quiet and still and filled with good companionship and shared interests.

What a fool. How wrong I was.

This, *this* was what I'd been missing. This spark of deep, dark need. This cavernous aching hole that Roy's kisses awakened within me. This greedy, gasping, awkward, messy, beautiful thing right here.

And now I had a taste, I wasn't at all sure how I'd give it up.

More. Give me more.

"We shouldn't," Roy muttered, his lips trailing kisses across my cheek to nibble at my neck. "We should stop."

"Why?" I asked, a moan slipping free.

"You're here to mend a broken heart. I'm the bodyguard, not the rebound."

I fisted my fingers in his hair, holding his lips to my neck. "Can't you be both?"

Roy's lips stilled, his body tensing.

Uh, oh.

He pulled back, searching my face, his expression unreadable.

"Is that what you want, Charlotte? A rebound?"

I opened my mouth only to find myself strangely tongue-tied.

"Maybe."

He growled.

"I mean...." I stuttered, confused by his reaction. "It's not as if you care about me."

Roy's hands let me go, my legs unwrapping as my body slid down his. Safely on the ground, he stepped back, putting space between us.

"Get your coat."

I raised my eyebrows. "What? Why?"

"We're going out."

"Where?"

He pointed at the view of the glittering town in the distance.

I watched him shrug his coat on and disappear outside, leaving me in the cabin with Phoebe.

I glanced at the dog. "Is he always like this?"

She sighed, rolling over to present her belly to me.

"I'll take that as a yes."

SEVEN
ROY

Polar Bear, Alaska

I'd made a mistake. A huge fucking mistake.

I sat across the booth from Charlotte, watching her flick through the menu as if it were the most fascinating thing she'd ever read.

"It says reindeer sausage? As in actual reindeer?" she asked, glancing up.

I nodded, watching her nose screw in response.

"Oh. No, thank you. I don't think I could stomach eating Bambi's mother." She returned to perusing her menu, her long fingers gently stroking the pages.

Damn. How is that erotic?

Her kiss had destroyed me. Years of

suppressed wanting had erupted, and I had no way of stemming the flow.

"What about fried—"

"I'll order." I stood abruptly, reaching for her menu.

"But I haven't decided."

I nodded at the board above the register. "Get the special. It's always good."

She read the menu, her head tilting to one side. "Alright."

The bar held a mix of booths and tables and specialised in fish, burgers, and beer. Barely more than a weather-proofed shack, the locals filled every table, such was the quality of the food.

I ordered, taking my time as I tried to get a handle on my emotions.

Dressed in a fluffy jumper with

"Who's the girl?"

I glanced over to find one of the locals watching Charlotte.

"None of your business."

Dawson laughed, leaning against the bar. "She looks like a tourist. You related?"

I snorted. "Do we look related?"

Dawson eyed me. "Maybe?"

I rolled my eyes. "No, we're not related. She's also Manari, but she's not a relative."

"That was racist, wasn't it?"

"A little."

"Sorry, bro."

I shrugged as the old bartender shoved my beers across the bar.

"She single?" The blond-haired, blue-eyed ladies' man gave Charlotte a once over.

"Not if you're asking."

"I am. I really, *really* am."

I walked away, ignoring Dawson's laughing protest.

Polar Bear had a woman problem. The men outnumbered the women by a vast majority, and as far as I knew, the only true single women in this place were either in diapers or old enough to be my grandmother.

"Who's your friend?" Charlotte asked when I slid back into the booth.

"Dawson."

She gave the guy a little wave. "Should we invite him over?"

"Fuck no." I handed her a beer. "Drink."

She took a sip, her eyes widening. "This is great."

"It's a local beer. The owner makes it himself."

She took another pull. "Does he export? I know some Hotelier's who'd kill to get their hands on this."

"Charlie, take a night off. You're here to

relax and lay low, not broker international trade deals."

She rolled her eyes. "Can't I do both?"

"I have no doubt you can. But let's wait until after dinner."

She sighed, turning to look out the window. "If you insist."

Our meals arrived shortly, beer-battered fish with thick-cut fries, fry bread, and roast veggies.

"Carb-heavy," she remarked, laying a napkin across her lap.

"Gotta be." I nodded at the snow outside. "You use up more energy during the winters trying to keep warm."

Charlotte hesitated, her dark eyes flashing with something unreadable.

"What?"

She shook her head. "I guess I never really thought about winter as a life-or-death situation. It's a far cry from our little Kingdom."

We began to eat, interrupted repeatedly as the men in the room wandered over to check out the town's newest attraction.

"Don't I know you?" One of the older timers asked, squinting at Charlotte.

"Not that I remember." She offered him a friendly smile. "But I've been told I have that kind of face."

He shook his head, my body tensing. "No, that's not it."

"I once won a pie-eating contest. The local papers published it back home."

Her gathered crowd of admirers laughed.

"No, no, not that." The old guy tapped the side of his head. "Wait! You're that girl."

I tensed, quickly assessing the situation.

"You're Moira's granddaughter."

I relaxed, forking the final bite of my fish.

Charlotte laughed. "No. But she sounds like a lovely person."

"She's not."

Charlotte's tinkling laugh rang out once again—and greedy fucker I was, I wanted to scoop her up and take her back to the cabin. I wanted to keep that all to myself.

"Wasn't she at the Plunge?"

"The plunge?" Charlotte asked, glancing at me.

"It's where people strip off and go splashing through the water. Some do it for charity, others for health."

"Naked? They go in there naked? During summer? It'd still be freezing wouldn't it?"

The locals shook their heads.

"Winter, my dear." The old-timer scratched his nose. "Tourists come just to participate."

"Winter?" She stared. "But surely you'd freeze!"

"There's definitely shrinkage," Dawson agreed. "But the upside is that you get longer life."

Charlotte laughed, waving her fork in the air. "I highly doubt that."

"You'd be wrong." He clapped the old guy on the shoulder. "John here is a hundred and eleven."

"Bull—" she swallowed her curse. "Lies. I don't believe it."

I sat back in my chair, watching her entertain the rowdy patrons, hating that they made her laugh but loving hearing it.

"You here for Christmas?" John asked.

"Uh, maybe." Charlotte worried her bottom lip.

"You know I don't do Christmas," I grunted, drawing the attention away from her.

"And yet you're putting up a woman who wears Christmas earrings." John shook his head. "Boys, I think we have our next bet. I'll put a five down that by this time next week there are decorations in his cabin."

"I'll take that."

Ignored the shouted wagers, I leaned in, brushing Charlotte's hair back to reveal her earring—for the first time noticing the tiny reindeer in Santa hats that decorated her earlobe.

"They're cute," she whispered, her gaze locked on my face.

I tangled fingers in her hair, unable to help myself. "We're not doing decorations."

Her full lips quirked, the corner of her mouth lifting into a half-smile. "What about a tree?"

"Absolutely not."

"Tinsel?"

"Fuck no."

"How about an ugly Christmas sweater?"

I shook my head, dropping back into my seat. "Charlie, we're not decorating the cabin."

She pouted, giving me big doe eyes. "Not even a little? What if I promise to do something for you in return?"

My gut clenched as I imagined her naked and spread on my bed.

"What something?"

She shrugged. "I don't know, clean your cabin? Wash Phoebe?"

Around us the crowd roared with laughter, a small chuckle even slipping free from me.

"Babe." I stood, tossing a tip on the table. "If you can successfully wash Phoebe without needing backup, I'll cut down the damn tree myself."

"And decorate it?" she asked, her expression hopefully.

"Charlie, I'll even wear a Christmas sweater."

She rose, holding out a hand for me to shake. "You have a deal."

I slid my palm against hers, relishing the contact.

What a pitiful life I lead.

I forced levity into my tone. "Easiest bet I ever won."

She grinned, her expression sharkish. "We'll see."

EIGHT
CHARLOTTE

Polar Bear, Alaska

I can do this.

I stared at Phoebe from my place on the bed, watching the giant dog watch me. Jetlag had caught up with me as we'd returned to the cabin, and I'd crashed out on the drive back. I didn't remember anything from the time we'd left the bar to waking up mid-afternoon, fully clothed but for my outer layer.

If Roy had slept beside me, he'd left no trace.

Infuriating man.

I wanted more kisses. I'd wanted to wear cute pajamas to bed that tempted him. I wanted to see that desperate, hungry look on his face.

Instead, I'd woken with crusty eyes, drool on my pillow, wearing day-old clothing. Roy had taken one look at me and disappeared outside, muttering something about the wood stack.

Showered, dressed, and with coffee and toast in my system, I was beginning to feel halfway to normal.

"Are you going to help me win this bet?" I asked Phoebe, grinning when her tail began to wag. "Yes, you are. You're a clever, gorgeous, powerful female who is going to support her fellow woman, aren't you?"

She whined, her tail wagging faster.

I stood, opening my arms. "Come here, pretty girl."

Needing no further invitation, the giant white fluffball raced across the room, throwing herself at me. With an oof, I fell back into the bed, the breath knocked from my lungs.

Note to self, this isn't a lapdog.

Roy had mentioned that she might be a Husky-Samoyed mix, but he'd never quite been sure. He'd adopted her from the pound when she was little more than a fluff ball that could fit in the palm of his hand.

"Not so little anymore."

I allowed a few minutes of mutual loving before gently pushing her off.

"Come on, beautiful girl. Let's get you prettied up."

I walked into the bathroom, Phoebe trailing me.

Roy didn't have a bathtub in his cabin but he did have a giant walk-in shower.

"Alright, my good girl, how are we going to do this?"

I considered my predicament, laying out a plan of attack.

Towels went down on the floors and surfaces. I shrugged off my clothing, slipping treats from my pocket into my hand as I walked into the shower.

"Come on, Phoebe," I coaxed, holding out my palm. "Come to Lottie, my darling."

If she could speak, I had no doubt she'd be telling me to fuck off. She plonked her ass on one of the towels, stubbornly ignoring my offered bribe.

"Okay, that's not gonna work."

What happened next could have been made into an 80's movie montage. I tried chasing her into the shower. I tried pushing her, pulling the towel, tricking her, laying a Hansel and Gretel like trail of treats.

Hell, I even tried manifestations.

"You are a strong, courageous woman," I told her, looking deep into her dark eyes. "You are brave, you are powerful, and you will conquer bath time."

She licked my nose but stubbornly refused to budge.

"Fine." I wrapped my arms around her, bracing for what was about to come. "We'll do it the hard way."

With a grunted heave, I lifted her into my arms, staggering into the shower stall and kicking the door shut.

She went wild, howling and squirming, desperate to get out.

"Phoebe!" I switched on the water, and armed with the shampoo and the showerhead, I approached the crazed beast, intent on winning my prize.

Christmas tree. Tinsel. Baubles. Presents.

Twenty minutes later, I heard a knock on the bathroom door.

"Charlotte? You okay in there?"

I switched the hairdryer off, smoothing a hand down my slightly damp shirt. "You make come in."

The door cracked open a fraction, Roy poking his head in.

"Are you—" His gaze dropped to Phoebe,

his eyes widening as he took in her fluffy, white, *clean* coat.

"I believe," I said, crossing my arms smugly over my chest. "You owe me a Christmas tree."

He blinked. "How did you—?"

"And decorations."

"Are you blow-drying her?"

"And a Christmas sweater."

Roy shook his head. "I can't believe it. I *don't* believe it."

I held out my arms, showing off my battle scars. "Believe it."

He crossed to me, his hands wrapping around my arms, his thumb grazing against the sensitive skin.

"She clawed you?"

I flushed under his scrutiny. "It was a mutual clawing."

He reached for the mirror, pulling the medicine cabinet open. "Let's get those patched up."

With gentle hands he applied antiseptic solution, examining each of the scratch marks to determine if it needed a band aid.

A funny, warm, gooey sensation bubbled cheerfully in my stomach, while a pleasant sensation tingled at the top of my scalp as he worked.

This man is dangerous.

"All done."

He said the words but his hands remained on my body, his fingers running gentle patterns across my hyper-sensitive skin.

I wanted him to kiss me again. I wanted him to take me to bed and make love to me. I wanted to experience everything I'd missed by settling for a damp cloth like Frederick.

Kiss me. Kiss me.

Kiss.

Me.

Roy cleared his throat, letting go of my arms.

"A bet is a bet," he said, his voice gruff. "If you want a Christmas tree, we should go now."

With that declaration, the infuriating man turned on his heel and left the bathroom.

I glanced down at Phoebe, rolling my eyes when I saw the towel nest she'd built for herself.

"Let's go Christmas tree shopping." I waggled a finger at her. "But no mud piles for you, young lady."

Her tail thumped enthusiastically against the floor, leaving me with little doubt she'd jump in the first mud heap available to her.

NINE

CHARLOTTE

Polar Bear, Alaska

We trudged through the calf-deep snow on the lookout for the perfect Christmas tree.

"What about this one?" Roy asked, pointing at a minuscule bush that barely came to his hip.

"No."

"This one?"

"With a bald spot? Absolutely not."

"This one?"

"No."

"What about—"

"There!" I pointed to the perfect tree, my heart leaping in my chest. "There she is."

At least seven feet tall with thick gorgeous foliage, the tree gave me actual goosebumps.

"Really?"

I nodded, clasping my hands together. "That's it."

"You sure you don't want to consider—"

"No, this is the one."

Roy eyed the fir. "You're sure?"

"A hundred and ten percent."

He sighed, scrubbing a hand over his face. "Good thing we brought the snowmobile. This thing is gonna be a bitch to get back."

I laughed, dancing around the tree. "But totally worth it. Look at her beautiful branches. Look at her span. Look at the trunk! Majestic! And, best of all, I looked it up, and you can replant after the holidays."

"Oh, joy."

I ignored his pessimistic attitude.

With much protesting, heaving, and a little swearing, Roy chopped down the beautiful fir. With practised hands, he wrapped the branches for safe transfer and hauled it onto a tarp for transport.

"Great job!" I said, shooting him thumbs up from my position on the mobile.

He grunted, swinging a leg over the snowmobile and whistling for Phoebe.

"Let's head home before this storm hits."

The wind kicked up as we headed back to the cabin, the heavy dark clouds rolling in at a terrifying rate.

"Get inside," Roy yelled, pushing me toward the cabin. "I'll get your tree."

My extremities freezing, I bolted inside, laying a fire and quickly swapping my soaked clothing.

I walked out of the bedroom to find Roy hauling the tree upright in a pot. Her branches flailed, pine needles dropping to decorate the floor.

While Roy wrestled her into place, I popped on the kettle, boiling some water for tea.

"That looks wonderful," I called, grinning as he managed to get the tree into a perfect position. "It's like she was always meant to be there."

He grunted in answer, pressing hands to his lower back as he straightened.

"Are you okay?"

"Fine."

I watched him kneed his back.

"Do you need a massage?"

Roy paused, his head slowly turning toward me.

"A what?"

"Massage." I held up my hands, wiggling my fingers. "If you're tight, I could help."

"No." His reply whipped into the air between us.

"But you're sore."

"I'm fine."

"Roy, let me help."

"No."

"But—" I rounded the couch, frustration building as he walked backwards away from me.

"I said no."

"Why?"

"Because I said no."

"But you're sore. Surely I can help."

"Charlotte—"

"Croydon—"

We both stopped, glaring at each other.

"You're hurting, let me help."

He crossed his arms over his chest. "I don't need your help. I'm perfectly capable of taking care of myself."

I rolled my eyes. "Of that, I have no doubt. But you dragged a tree into the house because of me. The least I can do is rub your back." I reached out, frowning when he ducked away from my hands.

"Croydon!"

"Don't touch me."

"But why? Why do you hate me?"

"Hate you? Hate you?" His face flushed, his eyes glittering. "I don't fucking hate you."

I threw my hands up. "Then why?"

"Because if you touch me, I'll never want you to stop."

I froze. "What do you mean?"

He stepped close, invading my space.

"You know exactly what I mean, Charlotte."

I stared at him, my mind blank as heat pooled deep in my core.

"Roy?"

He cocked an eyebrow.

Purposefully I laid a hand on his chest, my heart pounding as I invited danger into my life.

"Kiss me."

His gaze locked with mine, his jaw jumping.

"You sure?"

I nodded, licking my lips. "I want to feel exactly how you made me feel yesterday."

"What about your fiancé?"

"Ex-fiancé." I rose, leaning against him as I admitted my darkest secret. "The truth is, Frederick has never made me feel even an ounce of what you did yesterday."

Roy's big hand came up to cup the back of

my head, his expression fierce. "Don't lie to me, Princess."

"Never." I dropped one hand to press it against his cock. "Make love to me, Croydon. Make me feel wanted."

With a groan, he caught my lips—and with one scorching kiss, renewed my belief in love.

Oh, dear.

TEN
ROY

Polar Bear, Alaska

The want I'd felt since the moment I'd first seen her at the airport overpowered all rational thoughts.

I tasted her mouth, fingers fisting in her hair, tongue committing to memory every stroke and glide.

I want this woman.

"Charlotte...."

She blinked up at me, her lips swollen from our kiss, her eyes glazed with desire. My cock throbbed, desperate to know what she'd feel like as she came around me.

"Why did you stop?"

"Are you sure this is what you want?"

With deliberate slowness she pulled her sweater off, tossing it onto the sofa.

"I'm sure. Make love to me, Croydon."

Any finesse I might have possessed evaporated, my fingers clumsy as I hurried to strip her naked. As her clothes fell to the floor, the light from the fire began to warm her tawny skin, the satin feel of it an intoxicating addition to this already decadent feast.

My lips found hers, desperate for another kiss.

If I only have tonight then I better make it count.

In my heart, I knew a princess didn't marry the frog. And this frog wasn't about to turn into a prince—no matter how much I wished otherwise. But listening to her needy moans, feeling the silk of her skin, pulling druggy kisses from her swollen lips—I could almost convince myself that she could be mine.

Almost.

With a groan I stepped back, taking in her glory.

Triumphantly naked, she stood before the fire, the light licking her dark skin. Her breasts were full and heavy, her bronze nipples standing to attention. Her body curved and dipped, her hips wide, her waist trim. Her thighs were wide and welcoming, the kind of thighs that I hoped to wrap around my head as I tasted her sweet cunt.

I ripped my shirt off and dropped my hands to my fly, our gazes held while I stripped.

Naked, I watched her perusal of my own body, her cheeks flushing as she took me in.

Gods have mercy.

"I'm gonna taste your sweet pussy," I told her, my voice rough. "Then I'm gonna fuck you under this fucking tree."

She shivered, her tongue darting out to lick her lips.

"Then come do it, Roy."

I crossed the room, sweeping her into my arms and down onto the sofa. With a groan, I slowly kissed my way down her body, pausing to taste her neck, tease her breasts, press kisses across her hip bones.

I gently spread her legs, wedging my shoulders between them as my hands glided up and down her legs.

"You're soaked, Princess." I bent, brushing hot breath over her mound. Her scent teased me, and I had the sudden urge to coat my face in her juices. "I'm gonna taste you now, okay?"

She nodded, her breath coming out in an unsteady pant.

"Charlotte, tell me. This okay?"

She slowly blinked open dark eyes, her desire shining bright.

"Please," she whispered. "Please taste me."

I dipped my head, my fingers gentle as I parted her to reveal her most sacred place to my gaze.

Fuck.

I should have known she'd be perfect everywhere.

"Okay?" she asked, a note of anxiety in her tone.

"Fucking perfect." I rose to capture her lips in a slow, delicious kiss. "Just admiring your body. I've never seen anything so fucking perfect in my life. It's like you were made for me, Charlotte."

She melted into me, her hands coming to cup my cheeks.

"You're dangerous," she whispered, her hips shifting restlessly under my hands.

"Not to you," I promised, dropping back to my knees. "Never to you."

I bent, my tongue flicking out to capture the first glorious taste of her.

Fuck.

Under my mouth, Charlotte went wild. Her hands fisted my hair, her body bucking as I learned her wants and desires.

"Don't stop," she cried, holding me to her. "Oh, Gods. So good. So good!"

I chuckled, redoubling my efforts.

Don't worry, darlin'. I won't stop for anything.

I grazed my teeth across her sensitive skin, teasing and sucking, brushing and nipping, loving her breathy moans and startled sighs. I imagined myself a slave to her queenly desire, desperate to please the one woman in the entire kingdom who mattered.

When she was good and ready, I lifted a hand to press a finger against her, slowly dipping into her tight channel.

Charlotte's body arched, her hips riding my face with wild abandon as curses and praise fell from her lips in equal measure.

"Roy!"

I struck up a rhythm, stretching her out while my mouth concentrated on her clit.

"Roy, Roy, Roy...." My name became a mantra, Charlotte losing herself in the sensations I'd built in her.

"Come, Princess. Come for me."

I shifted, changing angles and pace, dark satisfaction unfurling as she broke apart under me, her lusty screams shaking the rafters of the cabin.

"Good girl," I praised, gently stroking her

body, waiting for her to come down. "That feel better?"

She nodded, unable to speak as she lay panting against my sofa.

"Mm, good." I continued to stroke her satin skin, revelling in her satisfaction.

"Roy?"

"Mm?"

Charlotte spread her legs wider, her gaze full of hunger. "You made me come, now let me return the favour.

I stilled, staring at her.

"What do you mean?"

"I want to taste you," she murmured her hips shifting to grind her pelvis against me. "Please."

Fuck.

I surged to a stand then bent, pressing a hard, desperate kiss to her greedy mouth. My thumbs raked over her nipples as we ravished each other's mouth, the taste of her pussy still sweet on my tongue.

"My turn."

I stepped back, allowing her to capture my cock.

"Don't make me come," I warned her, fisting her hair in one hand. "I want to fuck your tight cunt."

She shuddered, her eyelids drifting to half-mast. "I love when you talk dirty to me."

Good.

Charlotte shifted, licking her way down my stomach to my groin, her hands massaging my erection.

Fuck that feels good.

Her head dipped, her mouth closing around my dick. For a beat, neither of us moved, held suspended by the sweet torture of anticipation.

With a last glance up, Charlotte's eyelids drifted shut, her head and hands moving as she began to work me over.

"Fuck!" I swore, heat shooting through my cock. "Fuck. That's it, baby. Just like that. Work me, baby. Fuck my cock down your throat."

I love this woman. I fucking love her.

The thought wasn't new. I'd felt it for years as I'd watched her navigate her way through the most tragic of circumstances with poise, elegance, and cheer. She'd helped my tarnished heart feel lighter, bringing joy to my otherwise bleak existence.

Leaving had been the hardest goddamned thing I'd ever done. But I'd known I could never have her. Not with princes and diplomats and billionaires sniffing around.

Yet here she was, her mouth wrapped

around my cock, her taste on my lips. It defied belief.

Or perhaps she was right. Maybe those cookies were magic.

I reached down, hauling Charlotte up and into my arms.

"Roy! I'm not finished."

"Yes, you are." I settled her on the sofa, bending until I could hover over her. I fumbled for a second, getting the condom on then fisted my cock in my hand.

"Ready?"

She sucked in a breath, her eyes wide.

"Yes."

With gentle movements I found her core, arching back slightly to watch as the head of my cock bridged her sex, stretching her as I eased inside.

Fuck, she's tight.

"Oh, Gods. Oh, fuck." Her sweet muttered whispers fuelled my desire.

"Your pussy is heaven, baby," I whispered against the shell of her ear, slowly thrusting in and out. "You're so fucking tight. You're like a vice around my dick. You feel so fucking good."

At my whispered praise, she went wild, arching her hips, her thick thighs wrapping around me to give her better leverage.

I fed her more of my cock, quickening my pace.

"Take me, Princess. Let me fuck your sweet pussy. Let me stretch your tight cunt."

I stroked deeper inside her, groaning as she raked fingers down my back, her movements wild.

"More, more, more, more!"

"More? So greedy." I nipped at her bottom lip. "You ready?"

"Yes!"

I fucked her, rough and hard, giving her all of me. For a beat, I worried I'd overwhelmed her and pushed her too far.

Fuck.

Charlotte's head fell back, her inky hair spilling across the tan sofa, a low keening wail slipping from between her swollen lips.

"Roy...!"

Mine.

My cock throbbed, my balls drawing up as my climax began to bear down on me.

Charlotte's tight cunt spasmed as her orgasm tore through her, scorching us both. I erupted, fucking her into the sofa, my cock gripped by the vice of her clutching flesh.

I collapsed on top of her, knowing this would be a memory I'd take to my grave.

For a long moment, we lay panting together, the sweat cooling on our skin.

"Roy?"

"Mm?"

Charlotte grazed gentle fingers through my hair, holding me to her. "Can we do that again?"

I huffed out a laugh, pressing a kiss to her shoulder. "Fuck yes."

She sighed, relaxing under me. "Good."

I shifted, moving to give myself better access to her breasts. "Now good for you?" I sucked one delicious tip into my mouth.

"Oh." Her eyelids drifted shut, her body melting. "Only if you insist."

I grinned. "I abso-fucking-lutely do."

Polar Bear, Alaska

I leaned against the doorjamb, staring at Roy's naked ass.

Mine. That sexy goodness is all mine.

The last few days had been pure bliss. Full of joyful discovery and sexy laughter, I'd learned more about my body, my emotions, my soul in the last three days than in the past twenty-odd years of my life. It felt strange to admit that sex had freed me from a prison I'd allowed to be crafted around myself.

Roy may have been the catalyst, but I was the warrior woman who'd begun to break down the walls, determined to fight for what I wanted.

And what do you want, Charlotte?

The answer came easily. I wanted to leave behind the restrictions of my previous life. I wanted a small cabin in a freezing part of the world where a man and his dog lived. I wanted cosy nights making dinner, and long lazy days spent in bed. I wanted his whispered praise that sent shivers down my spine. I wanted Roy's grunts and grim expressions. I wanted his exasperation at my Christmas spending and his eye-rolls at my antics.

I wanted him under me and over me. I wanted to be exactly where he was.

Did that mean I'd abandon my duty? No. I wanted to continue my charity work, and see my family regularly, but overall I found myself craving more of the peace he'd brought to my life.

It'll never last.

I closed my eyes, fear washing over me.

I knew this little escape from reality wouldn't last forever. Life as a royal wouldn't permit me the freedom to just run off to the mountains regularly. But gosh did I wish it were so.

He'll never agree to be in the kind of spotlight you attract.

I sighed, wondering if this chemistry between us had the power to bloom into a life together. We were electric, burning up the

ELEVEN
CHARLOTTE

bedroom...and the kitchen... and the closet... and the shower... and his snowmobile.

But would we continue to spark? Or would these feelings fade to ash?

My heart ached, a pit developing in my stomach.

"I can hear you thinking," Roy growled from the bed. "And it doesn't sound like good thoughts." He lifted his head, the heat in his gaze warming my blood. "Why?"

I walked across the room to crouch on the bed beside him. Unhappy with the distance between us, he immediately intertwined our fingers, shifting us until I pressed into his side.

"What's wrong?" he asked, nuzzling my hair.

"Is this real?"

He paused, and I appreciated him taking a moment to consider my question.

"The quiet and escape from your paparazzi isn't. That will only last for a finite time." He dipped his head, bringing our joined hands to his lips. "But this is." He pressed a kiss to my fingers.

"Is it too soon? Is it too intense?"

He snorted, his beard tickling my fingers. "Fuck no. Sometimes, Charlotte, you gotta take a chance. You might have started this with your hot little pleas for kisses."

I giggled, dipping my head. He caught my chin, gently lifting my face to capture my gaze.

"But this isn't something I want to end. We're fantastic together, Princess. And as much as it kills me to know you'd be marrying under you, I want the chance. Not yet." he rushed on, capturing my stunned expression. "But one day. When you're ready."

I swallowed, stunned to find that the idea of a wedding didn't cause nearly as much anxiety as I expected.

"Would you get married on the grounds of the *Murmuranay*?" I asked, referring to our sacred meeting place. "And wear a *merimorini*? Would you perform the wedding dance?"

"Mah sagra," he murmured, brushing a kiss to my forehead. "Gladly."

I will.

"Our culture is a part of us, Charlotte." He shifted, pressing our hands to my chest. "Your spirit is tied to our home. And while these mountains might be nice to visit as an escape, but we both know that Astipia is our land. It's where we are called to be. It's where we'll live and grow. It's where we'll marry and raise children, and it's where we'll pass—returning to the land that birthed us."

Tears stung the back of my eyes.

"Make love to me."

"Gladly."

In the soft light of the morning, we touched and caressed. This time there was no frantic grasping, no surging desperate need.

This moment felt like two souls beginning to weave together.

Slow druggy kisses and long lingering touches. Gentle whispers, and murmurs of praise. We took our time, exploring each other, learning and relearning what brought pleasure.

And when it was over, Roy leaned down to cup my pussy.

"Hei garell," he whispered, pressing a kiss to my lips.

My only.

The words were normally reserved for wedding nights, the promise a sacred vow between lovers intending on binding their lives together.

Tears stung my eyes as I reached down, coating my fingers in my desire, touching the wetness to the skin above his heart.

"Hei garell," I repeated, sealing our promise.

I prayed to all the Gods this would last.

Polar Bear, Alaska

"Where's your man?" Dawson asked, sliding into the booth beside me.

I glanced up from the menu, grinning at the cute fisherman. "He needed to make a phone call."

Dawson reclined, on the seat, his lanky body taking up far too much space. I shifted, moving toward the big window, giving him more room.

"Did you win the bet?"

I grinned, tossing the menu onto the table. "I did indeed. We've just been decoration shopping, actually."

"I bet he was a right bear about it."

I laughed. "Absolutely."

We'd finally emerged from the cabin when the food had run out. After days spent wrapped in each other, it felt strange to be surrounded by others.

"Dawson," Roy greeted, staring down at his friend. "You wanna get out of my seat?"

The fisherman sighed, stepping out and sliding across to the other seat. "If I must."

Roy waited while he settled then sat beside me, his hand immediately linking with mine.

"All okay?" I asked, noting the tension in his shoulders.

His jaw twitched. "We'll talk about it later."

I stilled, not liking his tone.

"Should I be worried?"

"Not yet."

"You're cute together," Dawson interrupted, leaning back in the booth. "You been dating long?"

Roy's expression turned menacing. "Who said we were dating?"

He snorted, looking meaningfully between us. "You're barely keeping your hands off her. Don't bullshit me."

I flushed, glancing down at the table.

"A word of caution." Dawson shifted in his seat, leaning across the table, his voice dropping. "There's a reporter sniffing around the joint offering a rather large sum of money for the whereabouts of a runaway princess."

I sucked in a breath, turning to stare at Roy.

"Don't know any princesses," Roy commented mildly, his expression unreadable.

"Mm." Dawson pulled his phone free, swiping across the screen. "Strange that. I could swear I've seen Charlie's face before." He slid the phone across the table, the video already beginning to play.

In technicolour glory, the final moments of my previous relationship played out for all the world to see. A quick glance showed over a billion views.

Berryn must be losing his mind.

The video showed Fredrick backing up from the dais, his head shaking back and forth as he made a break for the doors of the church.

I closed my eyes, not needing a video to replay the scene.

"Where are you going?" I'd screamed down the church aisle, gathering my skirts and chasing after him. *"Fred!"*

He'd not answered, simply turned and run.

I'd caught him outside just as the caterers

*were passing with the wedding cake, setting up
for the reception that would never come.*

*"Frederick! Wait! Where are you going?
What's going on?"*

*"Away," he'd returned, barely glancing at
me. "It's over, Charlotte. We're done."*

"Done?"

*"I don't love you." He'd looked me in the
eye, delivering the words that had shattered the
lies we'd woven around our relationship. "And
you don't love me. This has all been a sham.
And I refuse to live it another moment longer."*

*Anger, hurt, shame—the death spiral of
emotions had erupted into a ball of insanity. In a
fit of rage, I'd smashed my hand into the passing
pastry, wound my arm back, and let the handful
of chocolate almond truffle cake fly.*

"She's got a good shot," Roy commented
mildly, handing the phone back to Dawson.
"You should write to her, and see if she'll join
your baseball team."

"A news network is offering a reward for
her whereabouts. Quarter of a million dollars."
Dawson shook his head. "A man could do a lot
with money like that."

My stomach clenched, my veins turning
to ice.

"You know, I've lost my appetite." Roy

tugged me to my feet, tossing bills on the table. "Thanks for the heads up. I'll catch you later."

"Later."

Roy led me from the bar, his steps unhurried and casual.

"Should I be wor—"

"Hush for a minute, babe. I need to think."

My mouth snapped shut, my hands holding fast to him. Once safely in the SUV, Roy finally spoke.

"The phone call was from the palace; they know about the reporters. Someone from the airport tipped them off."

I closed my eyes. "What happens now?"

Roy blew out a breath. "They think you should return home. You disappearing was a stupid idea. It's revved the press up. Everyone wants the first photo of the runaway princess."

"Damn."

We sat in silence, staring out at the snow-covered mountains.

"When?" I asked, my heart heavy.

"Tonight." Roy twisted, his expression clear. "A jet is on its way."

"Are you coming?"

Roy's eyes drifted shut. "I can't."

"Why? Why not?"

He pinched the bridge of his nose. "It'll be

a scandal, Charlotte. They'll accuse you of cheating. I won't have it."

My heart thundered in my chest, sweat dampening my palms. "But we know the truth. I don't care about everyone else. I care about us."

"I know, baby." He reached out, brushing a stray tear from my cheek. "But the palace recommended the pause. They don't want you hurt any more than I do."

"I don't care."

"It's for the best, babe. It'll only be a few months then we can be together."

"You promised," I whispered, my heart breaking. "You gave me the vows."

"And I intend to keep them. I swear it, Charlotte. Our life together has already started."

We returned to the cabin for my things—and made love on his bed for a final time. Desperate and clawing, I marked him over and over, leaving hickey's on his skin in a desperate hope that he'd remember me once I'd left.

Don't let this fade.

At the airport, Roy pulled me tight, bending to press a hot kiss to my lips.

"Just a few months," he promised, brushing stray hairs from my cheeks. "Then we'll be together."

"Swear it."

"You're hei garell, Charlotte. I swear."

With a final kiss, we parted, Berryn guiding me across the runway to the waiting jet.

I sat at the window, my heart breaking as I watched him get smaller and smaller until finally, the clouds obscured him from view.

Only then did I cry.

THIRTEEN
CHARLOTTE

**Royal Palace, Astipia
Christmas Eve**

"You're not yourself, my Charlotte."
I glanced up from the dinner table, finding my mother watching me.

"I'm fine," I lied, forcing a weak smile. "Just tired."

It had been two weeks since I'd last seen Roy, and despite texts and phone calls—and one very hot session of phone sex—I ached for him.

Mother paused, her lips pursing together as she considered me.

Around the dinner table sat Kit, Jon, and Leo. Each year we celebrated the night before

Christmas as the reigning Monarch's had many duties on the actual day.

"You miss him," she said, the conversation stilling.

I flushed under the scrutiny of my family. "I do."

"He's a good guy, Lottie. He'll stay true to you."

Leo's reassurance opened an ache in my heart.

"I know. But that doesn't change the fact he's a million miles away."

"Victoria, says it'll only be a few more months. Maybe even less if Frederick begins dating earlier," Kit remarked, breaking her bread roll in half.

Kit's executive assistant, Victoria, ruled the palace staff with an iron fist—making my sister's job that much easier.

"I know." I looked down at my plate, moving peas with my fork. "Just a few more months."

Was I being dramatic? Absolutely. But my heart didn't care. I wanted Roy. I wanted his big arms and his grump growls. I wanted laughter and teasing and watching him sneak Christmas cookies as if I wouldn't notice they were missing.

We didn't even get a chance to put up the

decorations.

My heart hurt imagining him and Phoebe and our beautiful but naked tree celebrating the loneliest Christmas ever.

A maid entered the room, bopping a curtsy before moving to Mother's side. She leaned in whispering something in her ear.

"Wonderful. Thank you, Lucy." Mother turned to the table, a large smile on her beautiful face. "The presents have arrived."

"Presents?" Leo asked, perking up. "We get presents?"

Mother gestured at Lucy who nodded, a conspiratorial smile on her face. She reached for the door to the dining room, throwing it open with a dramatic flourish.

For a beat I didn't register the man in the doorway, my thoughts too blocked by my wretched case of the sads.

"What?" Roy asked, holding his arms out wide. "No welcome?"

I stared at him, my heart leaping. "Roy?"

"Right here."

With a shuddering sob, I shoved back from the table, sprinting the short distance across the room to throw myself in his arms, wrapping tight around him.

"You're here!"

He laughed, crushing me in his arms. "Your

mother invited me. Said a Princess needed some happiness for Christmas."

I looked over my shoulder to find my family watching us.

"Thank you."

Mother chuckled. "Love might not recognise distance, but the head certainly does. I can't have my Charlotte sad on Christmas."

Roy let me slide down his body, pressing a quick kiss to my forehead before turning to bow to the gathered.

"Majesty."

Kit approached, wrapping Roy in a hug. "Welcome to the family, Croydon."

He grinned, accepting the hug. "Thank you. It's good to see you."

She stepped back, eyeing his sweater. "I wish I could say the same, but your fashion sense leaves much to be desired."

The Christmas sweater had to be the ugliest, most gaudy thing I'd ever laid eyes on.

I adored it.

Over her head, I met his gaze, my heart full.

"I lost a bet to the woman I love." He pressed something on the sweater, turning on the multiple flashing lights. "Gotta pay up."

With a watery sob, I reached for him once again, pulling him down to pepper his face with kisses.

"I love you too," I whispered, allowing him to brush tears from my cheeks.

"I know." He leaned in capturing my lips in a sweet kiss. "Merry Christmas, Princess."

"Our first of many."

With one last kiss, we rejoined my family—hand-in-hand.

EPILOGUE ONE

Charlotte

Polar Bear, Alaska
One year later

"But where will Leo sleep?" I asked, frowning at my fiancé.

"On the couch."

Leo had leave coming up and wanted to visit the cabin to 'ensure I was being looked after appropriately'.

I suspected it was a ploy to escape Kit forcing him into babysitting the tiny dictator.

I raised an eyebrow. "Phoebe sleeps on the couch. There'd be no room."

Roy stilled, a slight flush creeping up his neck.

"Uh, so about that." He strode across the cabin to begin tapping one of the walls. With a few tugs and tucks, he pulled the wall down to reveal a Murphy bed.

I blinked then blinked again.

"Croydon. That's a bed."

He nodded, one hand lifting to rub at the back of his head.

"Roy... it's a second bed. In our cabin." I stared at him. "You had a spare bed this entire time?"

His flush deepened. "Yeah."

Delighted by his deception, I bounced from foot to foot, clasped hands pressed to my chests. "You *lied.*"

He nodded, wincing.

"You fabricated a one-bed scenario to—" I paused, stilling. "Wait, why did you fabricate a one-bed scenario?"

He mumbled something I couldn't quite hear.

"What was that?"

He sighed, glaring at me. "I wanted to sleep next to you. Happy? I'd been fucking crazy about you, Charlotte. Even if I couldn't touch you, couldn't taste you—even knowing you weren't mine, I wanted to be beside you. I wanted the dream."

I melted. I knew I should likely be outraged

by such manipulative deception but I didn't care. I honestly didn't care. No, that's not true. I was overwhelmed with love for this sneaky, sneaky man.

I took a running leap, wrapping myself around him like a monkey, peppering kisses across his surprised face.

"Wait, you're not mad?" He asked, his hands gripping my ass.

"Nope." I squeezed him tight.

"Why?"

I rested my head on his shoulder, closing my eyes. "Because sometimes dreams come true. I hoped for a happy ending and you made that possible."

I pressed a kiss to his neck. "I love you, my sneaky, deceptive man."

I felt the tension release from his muscles. "And I love you, Princess."

I pulled back slightly, shifting until my mouth hovered just above his. "Shall we break in the bed?"

A grin stole across his lips. "If you insist."

"Oh, I definitely do."

We stripped, hands and mouths dancing across heated skin as we teased and stroked, desire burning bright between us.

Roy shoved me back onto the bed, standing before me like a ravishing mountain man.

"Can I taste?"

He blinked, his hand stilling.

"Please?"

"Fuck. Come here."

With a grin, I shuffled to the edge of the bed, fisting his cock.

"Ready?"

"Suck me, Princess."

I closed my mouth around the crown of his cock, my tongue lapping at the underside, moaning at the salty taste of his precum.

"Fuck, Charlotte. Your hot mouth feels incredible. Suck me, baby. Take me deep.

With a confidence that came from knowing exactly what he loved, I leaned in, taking him to the back of my throat, my hand dropping to play with his balls as I began to rock back and forth, coating his cock, teasing him.

With a moan he pulled back, my mouth releasing his cock with a pop.

"Oh, but I was having fun."

"Fun?" He pushed me back, covering my body with his. "I'll show you fun."

He rubbed his cock against me, teasing us both.

"Roy, stop teasing."

"But you love it." He sucked my nipple into his mouth, swirling his tongue against the erect tip. "Beg for it."

"Please, Roy. Please fuck me."

With a final swirl, he surged in, both of us groaning at the delicious friction.

"Fuck, babe. You're so tight."

"Kegels," I whispered, my eyes drifting closed. "Kit recommended it."

After the birth of her baby, she'd become obsessed with core and pelvic floor strengthening, terrifying me with tales of all the things that could go wrong.

"You ready?"

I moaned, nodding as my capacity to form words disintegrated.

Roy rocked against me, working me over, stretching me as he fucked hard and fierce.

Claim me.

"That's it, baby. Take me. Let me fuck you. Let me love you."

I clawed at his back as filthy praises fell from his lips, adding to my pleasure.

He built me up and set me on fire, fucking me until I exploded. I screamed, clawing at his back as I milked his cock, gratified when he came with a grunting, growling roar.

"Charlotte!"

We collapsed on the Murphy bed, panting as we

"I still can't believe you lied about the bed."

He grinned, raising on one arm. "Do you care?"

"Not even a little."

I closed my eyes, loving listening to him laugh as I thanked the Gods for sending such a sneaky man into my life.

EPILOGUE TWO

Charlotte

Grand Hall, The Royal Palace
Six months later

Unlike my first wedding where I wore a simple dress at the behest of Frederick, this time I wore a dress of ivory and lace and gems, the glittering, gorgeous concoction an ode to my fiancé's love for me.

Never diminish who you are, Princess. You're incredible.

The dress was made of Astipian fabric by Astipian hands. Kit had presented it to me with tears in her eyes.

"For you, my dearest sister. A dress fit for a queen."

Kit approached, laying a *merimorini*—a traditional wedding cloak— over my shoulders, shifting to tie it at my neck.

She stepped back and I stared at myself in the mirror, noting the flush on my cheeks and the smile that wouldn't quit.

I'm getting married.

Mother approached, fussing with the beautiful woven feather and dyed grass band that would wrap around Roy and me as we said our wedding vows.

"As I said to your sister, so I say to you. This merimorini has been worn by every woman who came before and will be worn by every woman who will come after you." She wrapped an arm around my waist, looking at us in the mirror. "It is my honour, daughter, to present this to you on your most special of days."

With gentle hands she turned me toward her, clasping my arm to her chest, pressing her forehead against mine. With a pounding heart, I listened as she whispered the words of blessing, words which were as old as time.

May your ancestors bless you and your chosen half. May your souls merge until there is no end and no beginning. May you be at peace, and dwell in love. May your years together be long. This is our wish for you.

Mother released me, stepping back as Kit took her place, reciting the blessing to me.

"Thank you," I whispered, tears stinging my eyes. "Thank you for supporting us."

"Darling." Kit reached up, brushing a finger across my cheek. "He's the man you were always meant to marry."

Mother stepped forward, laying a hand on my other cheek. "Let's not keep him waiting."

My heart leapt, anticipation sizzling in my stomach. With a last glance at the mirror, I turned, heading toward my future.

To Roy.

———

Roy

Jon slapped a hand on my shoulder.

"She's here."

I straightened, turning to look at the entrance to the garden, my heart beating out a tattoo of anticipation.

At the entrance, Charlotte paused to slip off her shoes, the small crowd silent as they watched her ready herself to enter this sacred place.

Barefoot on the sacred ground of

the *Murmuranay*, I shifted, desperate to claim her as mine.

Her head tilted back, her gaze meeting mine across the grove, her joyful spirit so bright I was surprised she didn't rival the sin.

My sunshine. My love. My wife.

To honour our heritage, I'd had the traditional marriage swirls inked into the skin on my wrists this morning, declaring for all the world I would only take this woman.

I saw Charlotte's gaze drop to my arms, her shoulders hitching.

Only you.

A drum began to pound, setting up the beat for the marriage chant. In a dance as old as time, one bare foot stepping in front of the other, Charlotte walked toward me, Leo at her side.

Her hair in a simple braid decorated with flowers and a small tiara, she looked like an angel.

Leo halted them halfway down the aisle, the drums falling silent.

"Wha me rundorni ma al oinp?" Leo shouted, pounding his chest in an even beat.

Who dares marry this woman?

I stepped forward, answering him with a beat on my chest. "Ma toaeria."

This warrior.

"Mala juni meta olpola?"

What is your bride price?

"Hei grahna, hei dilsna, hei katmu."

My love, my loyalty, my life.

Leo turned back to his sister, pounding once on his chest. "Ki mar alerni ma toaeria kelipu mun?"

Do you accept this warrior, my sister?

Charlotte's joyous shout startled a laugh from the crowd. "Mah sagra!"

I will!

Leo stepped back, pounding one fist over his heart as the crowd took up the beat.

Unassisted, unhindered as was required by the Gods, Charlotte came to me, taking my hands in hers as we turned to face the elder.

Kihana Mary, the woman who'd married Kit and Jon, called the ceremony to order and began the traditional blessing, commencing the wedding.

"We meet on this sacred place to marry two lovers, uniting them under the eyes of the Gods, and on the land of our ancestors." She swept a hand out, encompassing the forest surrounding. "The *Murmuranay* is known in our culture as a meeting place. A place that straddles two times, the before and the after. It is here where births are celebrated, and deaths are mourned. And it is here where our lovers will pledge themselves to each other. These are two who shall become one. They will be partners, they will become each other's lives, the other half of each other's soul."

She looked beyond us to Kit.

"You may now cloak them in the *merimorini*."

Charlotte and I clasped fists, stepping into each other to trap our arms between our bodies, our foreheads pressing tight as Kit used the woven grass belt to wrap the large merimorini around us.

"I love you," I whispered fiercely.

"And I, you."

A wave of possessive need hit me, and I fought a nearly overwhelming desire to throw her down and claim her on this hallowed ground.

Jon had warned me that the ceremony might provoke a primitive response—and fuck if he wasn't right.

We recited our vows, declaring our love, our loyalty, and our spirit to each other before the Gods.

"You may kiss the bride."

I captured her lips, hungering for a taste of her, gratified to find her just as desperate.

Grateful for the small amount of privacy the large *merimorini* offered, I pulled back, pressing my forehead to hers as applause washed over us.

"You got the tattoos," Charlotte whispered, tracing a finger over the angry skin.

"You planning on taking another husband?"

She grinned, shaking her head.

"Good. Cause you're stuck with me." I moved in, my lips hovering just a fraction above hers. "And I only plan on loving one wife for the rest of my life."

She melted into me, her body pliant. "I love you."

"And I love you, my princess."

With a final kiss, we sealed our fate—and began the next chapter of our happily ever after.

***

Thank you so much for reading Charlotte and Roy's love story! This one started off as a fanfic of Keeley and Roy from Ted Lasso and became its own thing!
I hope you enjoyed!

Be sure to sign up for my newsletter for more information on new releases, freebies, and teasers.

You can continue the entire series by checking them out on my website at www.EvieMitchell.com

*If you enter the code **EBOOK10** you can get 10% off your purchase from my website.*

ABOUT THE AUTHOR

Hey, I'm Evie Mitchell.
I'm a thirty-something romance author (she/her/hers) living with disability. I believe in inclusion, accessibility, and fierce romance. My loves include steamy romance novels, my sexy husband, our THREE sausage dogs (THE FUR!!!), and my ever-growing collection of book-related mugs.

As a woman with a diverse work history, including in areas such as hospitality, retail, emergency response, event management, human rights, disability access, and security— my books are filled with true stories (bridezillas), worst-case scenarios (malfunctioning zippers), and my favorite tropes (one-bed).

I'm a strong proponent of #OwnVoices, and specialize in fiercely inclusive happily ever afters.

EvieMitchell.com
Socials: @EvieMitchellAuthor

As You Wish

You Sleigh Me

Meat Load

Resolution Revolution

Dogg Pack

Puppy Love

Bad English

The Frock Up

Pier Pressure

Trick or Trent

New Year's Faye

Reigning Hearts

The Marriage Claim

Men of Trinity Bay

Kink in the Road

Nameless Souls MC

Runner

Wrath

Ghost

Shield

Elliot Security

Rough Edge
Bleeding Edge